First published as *Ridder Tim wil een draak* in Belgium and Holland by Clavis Uitgeverij, Hasselt – Amsterdam, 2017
English translation from the Dutch by Clavis Publishing Inc., New York

Visit us on the Web at www.clavisbooks.com.

Sir Tim Wants a Dragon written by Judith Koppens and illustrated by Eline van Lindenhuizen

ISBN 978-1-60537-369-0

This book was printed in April 2018 at Publikum d.o.o., Slavka Rodica 6, Belgrade, Serbia.

First Edition
10 9 8 7 6 5 4 3 2 1

Sir Tim
Wants a Dragon

Written by Judith Koppens
Illustrated by Eline van Lindenhuizen

Clavis

NEW YORK

"Mom," Tim calls, excited. "You told me I can get a pet, right?"

"Yes," says Mom. "As long you take good care of it."

"Look! I know what I want." Tim points to his book.

"I want a DRAGON!"

"A dragon?" Mom asks.

"All knights have dragons," Tim says.

"I'm a knight, so I need a dragon!"

"Come on, Mom. Let's go to the pet shop to buy my dragon!"

"Yes, but . . ." Mom says with a sigh.

"I don't think they sell dragons at the pet shop, you know."

But Tim has grabbed his cape and is already heading toward the door.

"Okay, Tim," says Mom when they get outside.
"We'll go to the pet shop so you can see for yourself
that they *really* don't sell dragons."
But Tim doesn't hear her.
He is running ahead with his dragon book
firmly under his arm.

"Hello, mister," says Tim when they get to the pet shop.
"My name is Sir Tim and I would like a dragon."

"Oh, young man,"
the shopkeeper says with a laugh.
"I don't sell dragons."
"Yes, but this book says that dragons
are animals," Tim protests.
"And you sell animals.
I want a DRAGON, please."

Then the shopkeeper sees that Tim is being serious.
"Um, let's have a look, shall we . . . ?
How about a turtle? A turtle is green like a dragon."
"Yes, Tim," Mom says. "A turtle is nice."
"No, a turtle isn't fast enough," Tim says sternly.
"I want a DRAGON!"

"A rabbit, maybe?" the man suggests.

"A rabbit is fast."

"Yes, and soft, too," says Mom.

"No, a rabbit isn't dangerous enough," Tim sighs.

"I want a **DRAGON!**"

"A mouse?" the man then suggests.

"A mouse has sharp teeth,

just like a dragon, and it's fast, too."

Mom is silent and makes a face. (She's not a big fan of mice.)

"No, no, no!" Tim says impatiently.

"A mouse is much too small.

I want a DRAGON!"

"Phew! I'm all out of ideas, then,"
the shopkeeper says with a sigh.
"That's all right," says Mom.
"Thank you for your time."
Tim takes Mom's hand and leaves the pet shop,
disappointed. He was so looking forward
to having his own DRAGON.

"Wait a minute, Sir Tim,"
the shopkeeper calls after them.
"I might just have what you are looking for after all . . ."

Tim and Mom go back inside.

"Look!" the shopkeeper says.

"I'd forgotten all about him."

Sir Tim gives the man a questioning look.

"That's not a DRAGON. That's a puppy."

"Yes," the shopkeeper says. "But his *name* is DRAGON.
And he wants to live with a nice knight like you."
Dragon licks Tim's face.

Tim looks up at Mom.

"Can Dragon come home with us, please?" he asks.

"Yes, I suppose he can," Mom laughs.

"I'm sure you will take good care of him."

"You see, Mom?" Tim says proudly.
"I found my **DRAGON** after all."
And Sir Tim and his dragon run right home.